9/700

D0579205

A F R I C A
BROTHERS AND SISTERS

by Virginia Kroll
pictures by Vanessa French

Four Winds Press ❄ New York

Maxwell Macmillan Canada   Toronto   Maxwell Macmillan International   New York   Oxford   Singapore   Sydney

Text copyright © 1993 by Virginia Kroll
Illustrations copyright © 1993 by Vanessa French
Four Winds Press
Macmillan Publishing Company
866 Third Avenue
New York, NY 10022
Maxwell Macmillan Canada, Inc.
1200 Eglinton Avenue East
Suite 200
Don Mills, Ontario M3C 3N1
Macmillan Publishing Company is part of the
Maxwell Communication Group of Companies.
First Edition
Printed and bound in the United States of America

10 9 8 7 6 5 4 3 2 1

The text of this book is set in Hiroshige.
The illustrations are rendered in watercolor and colored pencil.
Book design by Christy Hale.

Library of Congress Cataloging-in-Publication Data
Kroll, Virginia L.
Africa brothers and sisters / by Virginia L. Kroll ; illustrated
by Vanessa French. — 1st ed.
        p.   cm.
Summary: At lunchtime Daddy and Jesse play their favorite game: a
question and answer game about people who live in Africa and the
ways in which they are connected to Jesse.
ISBN 0-02-751166-9
[1. Fathers and sons—Fiction. 2. Afro-Americans—Fiction.
3. Blacks—Fiction. 4. Africa—Fiction.] I. French, Vanessa, ill.
II. Title.
PZ7.K9227Af   1993
[E]—dc20   91-20346

For my father, Lester Kroll, my original storyteller

—V.K.

Dedicated to my aunt, Julia M. Willis (1927-1990), and special thanks for the love and support of my husband, Nate, my parents, my sister and brother, and my nephew, who sat still

—V.F.

W hy don't I have any brothers or sisters?"
asked Jesse, knowing exactly what Daddy would say.

"You do," Daddy answered as he always did. "Dozens
of brothers, hundreds of sisters, thousands of Africa
brothers and sisters."

Jesse sat back to listen.

"Some are teachers and some are engineers," Daddy began.

"And businessmen like Uncle Charlie," Jesse continued.

"Yes," Daddy said, "and some
live in the city."
"Just like us," said Jesse.
"Just like us," Daddy said.

"Some of your Africa brothers and sisters are Ibo,"
Daddy told Jesse.

"Are they the yam growers?" Jesse asked.

"Many people grow yams," Daddy said with a twinkle
in his eye.

"But the Ibo are known all over Africa because they
grow the biggest, orangest, most delicious yams in the
world," Jesse said. "Yum, I love sweet potatoes!"

Daddy smiled his biggest smile, pleased that Jesse
remembered.

"Some of your Africa brothers
and sisters are Ashanti," Daddy
went on. "They weave beautiful,
colorful cloth with special designs
for all their people to wear for
celebrations."

"Maybe," Jesse said, "that's why
I love getting dressed up for parties
and holidays."

"Maybe," Daddy said.

9

"Tell me about my Africa brothers, the Guere," Jesse begged.

"They carve marvelous, often monstrous masks out of wood to wear during their dances," Daddy said.

"*Ooooh*," Jesse said in a scary voice. "I like monster faces."

Daddy rippled his voice and pulled his mouth into a ghastly grin. "Me *tooooooo!*"

Jesse sat up straight on the couch. "Don't forget the Djerma," he said sternly.

Daddy put a finger to his chin and cocked his head, pretending not to know. "The Djerma, the Djerma…"

"And don't forget the Falasha, Daddy," said Jesse.

"Hmm, the Falasha, the Falasha…"

"The Djerma make jewelry out of gold and silver, and the Falasha make pottery!" said Jesse.

"Yes," Daddy said. "The Falasha's ancestors molded pots and dishes and bowls from the earth by hand."

"They like working with modeling clay and so do I," said Jesse, showing Daddy his clay giraffe.

"And you're good at it too!" said Daddy.

"Who are my dancing Africa brothers and sisters?" Jesse asked.

"Almost all your Africa brothers and sisters are dancers," Daddy answered. "But the Keiyo, for instance, dance for days at celebrations. And then there are the Vai and the Ewe, whose drums 'talk' in remarkable rhythms."

Daddy tapped his hands on the coffee table, and Jesse joined in the beat.

"And who are the acrobat dancers?" Jesse asked.

"They are the talented, agile Dan."

"Daddy, I want to go to Africa."

"Someday you will," said Daddy.

"I bet I'd fit right in," Jesse said.

"And what about the artistic Baoule, Bamouns, and Benins?" Daddy asked, knowing how Jesse would answer.

"The three B's. I like art too," Jesse said, remembering his projects that Mrs. Low hung on the wall.

"Don't forget your thousands of Africa farming brothers and sisters," Daddy said.

"They grow corn and coffee and peanuts and things I never heard of," said Jesse.

"Like what?" Daddy asked.

"Like sorghum and millet," Jesse said.

"See, you *have* heard of them," Daddy teased. "Some of your Africa brothers and sisters are animal herders," Daddy continued, "like the Jie and the Masai with their cattle."

"Let *me* name some!" Jesse interrupted. "The Fulani and the Kirdi and the Dinka."

"Wonderful," said Daddy.

19

"What about the Wagenia?" asked Daddy.

"They're fishermen," said Jesse.

"Do the Sherbro fish too?"

"In long canoes with huge nets!"

"Umm, all of this talk makes me hungry. Shall we have lunch?" Daddy suggested.

"Yes," Jesse answered. "Let's have fish."

"Tuna fish it is," said Daddy.

"Tell me about the turbaned ladies," Jesse said, "the ones Mama looks like."

"They are the Wolof, your Africa sisters from the west. They wind bright, printed fabric round and round in a certain way, high atop their heads."

"Did Mama learn that from them?"

"They're the ones. She watched how they wound their head scarves, and now she can do it too."

"You and I wear hats," Jesse said.

Daddy grabbed his hat from the nearby rack and placed it on Jesse's head. "Yes, dapper gents that we are," he said.

"Are the Zulu the ones who weave fine baskets?" Jesse asked.

"Oh, many people in Africa weave fine baskets," said Daddy slyly.

"I mean the *finest* baskets, Daddy, the ones that can even hold water without leaking." Jesse got up and took a basket from the table. "Like this one." He showed it to Daddy.

"That's a Zulu basket, all right," Daddy said, "a cherished one."

"I know," said Jesse, "a souvenir from your honeymoon trip. When I go to Africa, I'm going to learn how to weave like that."

Jesse saved his favorite part for last. "And who are my Africa brothers and sisters, the best storytellers in the whole wide world?"

"They are the gifted griots from all over Africa," Daddy said. "When people hear their tales they come back over and over to hear more."

"That's probably why we both love this game," said Jesse.

Daddy sat back with a proud, happy smile. "Could very well be," he said. "Could very well be."

Here is a guide to help you pronounce the names of the tribes
Daddy and Jesse talk about in this book.

Ibo (EE boh)   Benin (beh NIN)

Ashanti (uh SHAHN tee)   Jie (GEE uh)

Guere (GEHR ruh)   Masai (mah SIGH)

Djerma (JUR mah)   Fulani (foo LAH nee)

Falasha (fah LAH shah)   Kirdi (CUR dee)

Keiyo (KEY oh)   Dinka (DING kah)

Vai (vy)   Wagenia (wuh GEN ee ah)

Ewe (EH vay)   Sherbro (SURE broh)

Dan (dan)   Wolof (WOH loff)

Baoule (BAH oo lay)   Zulu (ZOO loo)

Bamoun (BAH mun)   *griot (GREE ot *or* GREE oh)

Griot is not the name of a specific tribe. Griots are storytellers,
and they belong to many tribes all over Africa.

A NOTE FROM THE AUTHOR

Jesse and his daddy often play the game they play in this book to get to know their "brothers and sisters" of African cultures. Today they talked about twenty-one different peoples, but there are many, many more that Jesse and Daddy mention on other occasions.

For instance, they sometimes talk about their brothers and sisters from East Africa, including the Turkana (toor KAH nah) and the Samburu (SAM boo roo), who are animal herders; the Karamojong (CARE moh johng), whose men are famous for their hairstyles; the Kikuyu (kih KOO yoo), who place great emphasis on cooperation among their people; and the Swahili (swah HEE lee), whose name means "coast dwellers."

Jesse and Daddy discuss the herders and farmers called Galla (GAL lah), the Afar (AH far) nomads of Northeast Africa, and the Mbuti (em BOO tee) people of the Ituri (EE too ree) Rainforest.

The Somali (SO mah lee) and the Rendille (wren DEE lee) originate from the horn of Africa. The Xhosa (KOH suh), Ndebele (en deh BEE lee), and Sotho (SOO too) are Jesse and Daddy's sisters and brothers from South Africa.

Jesse and Daddy are becoming acquainted with desert peoples, including the Bushmen with their *click* language, the !Kung (KOONG), who carry water in ostrich eggshells, and the Tuareg (TWA reg), who are called the "people of the veil."

From West Africa come the Yoruba (YO roo bah), Dogon (daw GAWN), and Kongo (KAHNG goh) peoples, many of whom are farmers; the Hausa (HOW sah), famous for their proverbs; and the Malinke (mah LING kee), known for their strong musical heritage.

There are scores of others.

The more Daddy and Jesse study Africa, the more they learn that although some tribes are called "farmers," for example, it does not mean that they are *only* farmers. Today many of their Africa brothers and sisters hold to their rich, varied traditions and have modern jobs, too, just like people in countries all over the world.

And Jesse hopes that sometimes his brothers and sisters in Africa sit on their parents' laps and ask about *their* brothers and sisters—just like him—in America.

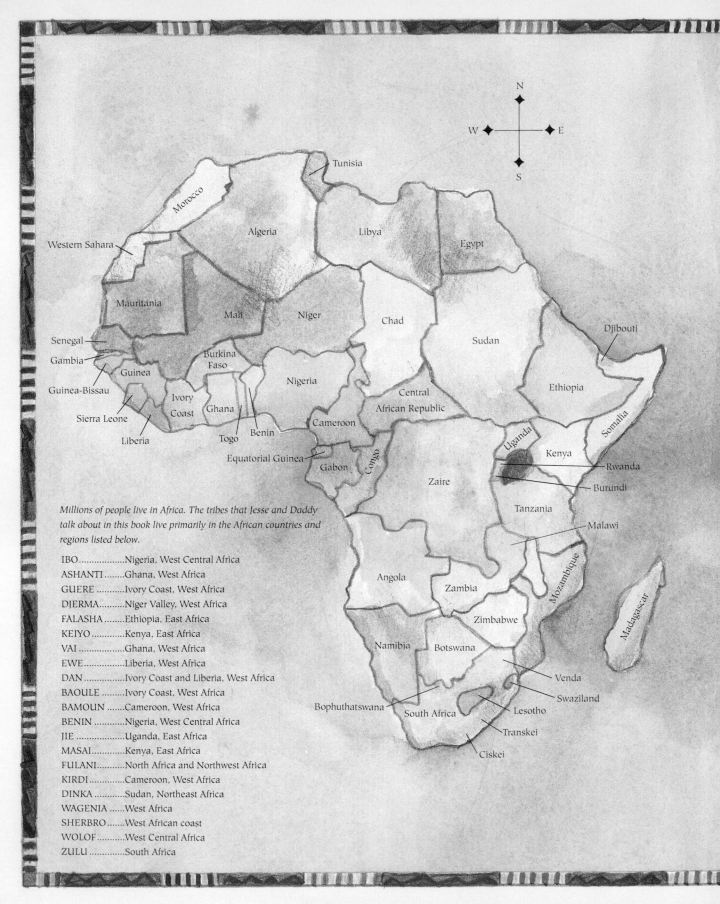

N
W   E
S

Tunisia
Morocco
Algeria
Libya
Egypt
Western Sahara
Mauritania
Mali
Niger
Chad
Sudan
Djibouti
Senegal
Gambia
Guinea
Burkina Faso
Nigeria
Ethiopia
Guinea-Bissau
Ivory Coast
Ghana
Central African Republic
Somalia
Sierra Leone
Liberia
Togo
Benin
Cameroon
Uganda
Kenya
Equatorial Guinea
Gabon
Congo
Zaire
Rwanda
Burundi
Tanzania
Malawi
Angola
Zambia
Mozambique
Madagascar
Zimbabwe
Namibia
Botswana
Venda
Swaziland
Lesotho
Bophuthatswana
South Africa
Transkei
Ciskei

Millions of people live in Africa. The tribes that Jesse and Daddy talk about in this book live primarily in the African countries and regions listed below.

IBO ....Nigeria, West Central Africa
ASHANTI ....Ghana, West Africa
GUERE ....Ivory Coast, West Africa
DJERMA ....Niger Valley, West Africa
FALASHA ....Ethiopia, East Africa
KEIYO ....Kenya, East Africa
VAI ....Ghana, West Africa
EWE................Liberia, West Africa
DAN ....Ivory Coast and Liberia, West Africa
BAOULE ....Ivory Coast, West Africa
BAMOUN ....Cameroon, West Africa
BENIN ....Nigeria, West Central Africa
JIE ....Uganda, East Africa
MASAI.............Kenya, East Africa
FULANI...........North Africa and Northwest Africa
KIRDI ....Cameroon, West Africa
DINKA ....Sudan, Northeast Africa
WAGENIA ......West Africa
SHERBRO ....West African coast
WOLOF...........West Central Africa
ZULU ....South Africa